KAY THOMPSON'S ELOISE

Eloise and the Snowman

STORY BY **Lisa McClatchy**

ILLUSTRATED BY **Tammie Lyon**

Ready-to-Read

Simon Spotlight

New York   London   Toronto   Sydney   New Delhi

SIMON SPOTLIGHT
An imprint of Simon & Schuster Children's Publishing Division
1230 Avenue of the Americas, New York, NY 10020
First Simon Spotlight hardcover edition September 2016
First Simon Spotlight paperback edition December 2011
First Aladdin Paperbacks edition October 2006
For information about special discounts for bulk purchases, please contact Simon & Schuster
Special Sales at 1-866-506-1949 or business@simonandschuster.com.
The text of this book was set in Century Old Style.
Manufactured in the United States of America 0816 LAK
2 4 6 8 10 9 7 5 3 1
The Library of Congress has cataloged a previous edition as follows:
Library of Congress Cataloging-in-Publication Data
McClatchy, Lisa.
Eloise and the snowman / story by Lisa McClatchy ; illustrated by Tammie
Lyon. — 1st Aladdin Paperbacks ed.
p. cm. — (Kay Thompson's Eloise) (Ready-to-read)
Summary: When snow starts falling in New York City, Eloise skips breakfast to rush out to
Central Park to build a snowman.
[1. Snowmen—Fiction. 2. Snow—Fiction. 3. Plaza Hotel (New York, N.Y.)—Fiction.
4. New York (N.Y.)—Fiction.] I. Lyon, Tammie, ill. II. Thompson, Kay, 1911–
III. Title. IV. Series. V. Series: Ready-to-read.
PZ7.M47841375E1 2006
[E]—dc22
2005030957
ISBN 978-1-4814-6748-3 (hc)
ISBN 978-0-689-87451-2 (pbk)

I am Eloise.
I am six.
I live at The Plaza Hotel
on the tippy-top floor.

This is my room.
If I am very, very careful,
I can peek out my window.

It is snowing!

"Nanny," I say,
"we must go outside."
"Not now, Eloise,"
   Nanny says.
"It is time for breakfast."

"Breakfast can wait,"
I say.
Oh, I love, love,
love snow.

We cross the street
to Central Park.

I roll a ball of snow.
I roll another . . .
and another.

"Look, Nanny," I say.
"It is a snowman."

But something is missing.

I hail a driver
and his horse.
"To The Plaza at once,"
I say.

"Room service," I say,
"please bring me one carrot."

I race back to the snowman
and Nanny.

"Nanny," I say,
"do you like his nose?"
"Oh yes, dear," says Nanny.

But something is missing.

"Driver, away," I say.

Only the best tailors will do.
I get a hat, a coat,
a scarf, and gloves.

"Nanny, how does my snowman look?" I say.

"Dashing, dear," says Nanny.
But something is missing.
"Back to The Plaza," I say.

"Eloise," says the manager.
"How may I help you?"

"We must build my snowman
a house," I say.
"Send me
your best carpenters."

"Eloise, dear, his house
is lovely," Nanny says.

But something is missing.

My breakfast.
"Nanny, let's go home,"
I say.

Oh, I love, love, love snow.